Oliver, ⬛ and Lar⬛

ORCHARD BOOKS
338 Euston Road, London NW1 3BH
Orchard Books Australia
⬛evel 17/207 Kent Street, Sydney, NSW 2000

ISBN 978 1 84616 300 5

First published in 2013 by Orchard Books

Text and illustrations © John Butler 2013

A CIP catalogue record for this book
is available from the British Library.

1 3 5 7 9 10 8 6 4 2

Printed in China

⬛ Books is a division of Hachette Children's Book⬛
an Hachette UK company.
www.hachette.co.uk

If Your Dreams Take Off And Fly

John Butler

ORCHARD

When the night is very dark
And the moon is shining high,
Let your dreams take to the skies
Like a dancing butterfly.

You will travel to a place
Where koalas you will see,
And kangaroos and platypuses
Running wild and free.

Then you'll leave them all behind,
As you flutter to the sky,
Looking for adventure,
My little butterfly.

Out across the oceans,
Watching whales as you pass by,
With all the world beneath you
Your dreams go flying high.

Then floating over icebergs,
Where the icy, cold winds blow,
You'll see penguins as they huddle
Finding shelter in the snow.

And when you reach the desert,
Where warm winds blow the sand,

There'll be a baby camel
Trotting out across the land.

Over grasslands and full rivers
You'll be floating in your dream,
While a family of hippos
Will be playing by a stream.

Drifting over forests,
As swallows swoop so fast,

A squirrel and a dormouse
Will watch as you glide past.

Then, flitting one last time
In the yellow setting sun,

You'll hear the sound of songbirds
As their lullaby is sung.

You will see so many things
And you will realise why,
Like you, this world is precious,
My little butterfly.

Our world is full of wonder
And your journey's just begun.
All you see around you
Is there for everyone.

And now it's time to sleep
But remember, if you try,
Anything can happen
If your dreams take off and fly.